Dead Issue
C. D. Moulton

Det. Clay Fordham was called when a boat burned off Sandy Point. There was a body aboard. Sam Boars, a man running for mayor on an anti-corruption platform.

It would have been listed as accidental – except for the two bullet holes in the corpse.

Contents

About the author

CD Moulton has traveled extensively over much of the world both in the music business, where he was a rock guitarist, songwriter and arranger and in an import/export business. He has been everything from a bar owner to auto salvage (junkyard) manager, longshoreman to high steel worker, orchid grower to landscaper, tropical fish farmer to commercial fisherman. He started writing books in 1983 and has published more than 350 books as of January 1, 2023. His most popular books to date are about research with orchids, though much of his science fiction and fantasy work has proven popular. He wrote the CD Grimes, PI series, and the Det. Nick Storie series, Clint Faraday series, and many other works.

He now resides in Gualaca, Chiriqui, Panamá, where he writes books, plays music with friends, does research with orchids and medicinal plants. He has lately become involved in fighting for the rights of the indigenous people, who are among his closest friends, and in fighting the extreme corruption in the courts and police in Panamá.

He offers the free e-book, *Fading Paradise*, that explains what he has been through because of the corruption.

CD is the discoverer of the Chadam Protocol for curing cancer.

Facebook page Ambrosia peruviana for cancer.

<u>*Lazy Afternoon*</u>

Clay Fordham, local police officer, sighed and poured another glass of lemonade onto fresh ice. Tim Weatherby, his one officer on duty, held out his glass for a refill. It was a peaceful lazy day. The view from the back porch of the office over the Pacific was beautiful and serene.

A boat went past a few hundred feet offshore. Lily and Gene Johns. They waved.

Clay and Tim talked about the difference in the area towns. Mayor Hank Fields spent one day a week at his job. Things were the way everyone wanted them. He was mayor because he was a proven administrator and was liked by almost everyone. There was no hint of scandal around him or his office – or the police.

Mayor Williams of Grandvista spent five and a half days at his job. Permits and such were handled by a staff of nine people. There were charges of corruption and worse against more than half the people employed by Grandvista

A fancy boat pulled into the dock at the gasolene/diesel pumps. There was some kind of banner flag in back.

"Politician," Tim said sourly.

"From Granvista," Clay replied. "Why can't they stay there? Why come here to campaign where no one can vote for them, anyhow? Boars isn't even county. He's just Grandvomit."

Everybody in Seaview knew everyone else. There were only two thousand three hundred people in the area. It was what was called "upscale." The difference between this and Grandvista, just nine miles away, was that these were mostly good friendly people. Grandvista was a collection of snobs. The people here were both comfortable and solvent. The people in Grandvista were generally in debt so far over their heads they would never recover.

"Seaview people live in houses they own while Grandvista lives in houses the banks own," was the way it was often stated. In Seaview, "We can go in my car." In Grandvista, "We can go in the loan company's car."

The two towns were very much the same size. Here, four total police officers and almost no crime. Grandvista, twelve police officers and a high crime rate, though much of their crime was white collar.

These people were real. Grandvista was a facade. It was that simple.

The boat went out into the Pacific about a

quarter mile and was going on down the coast. Clay shook his head.

Sandra Knowles came through the office to the porch and greeted them. She said Hank said for them to tell her whether she could use the park for a flower show. They could give her a permit or whatever.

Clay shrugged. "That's what the park's for. I'll give you a note."

"Oh, Dan and Flo and Frank will sell some things. I think we have to get a permit if there will be sales."

"The orchid and exotic fruit people? Permission will be on the note. You have to leave the park clean."

They chatted awhile about various things. The upcoming election didn't affect them much, but they had to have a vote because of the county and state crap. Hank was mayor and was going to stay mayor unless and until he walked out.

They spent the next couple of hours walking around the town. If anyone went to the office they would pick up the radio and call them.

Clay warned Levin, the owner of a general store, to keep his cardboard boxes and packing Styrofoam off the sidewalk and stopped at the Hilltop Lounge to warn Speedy that there were some minors from Grandvista who had false IDs. Tim told a traveling preacher, The Right Reverend O'Mally, to keep the volume down to 52 decibels at the property line or he would be cut off entirely. O'Mally tried to argue that there was no volume high enough when it came to The Lord's work.

"Matthew six. Don't hand me that crap," Tim countered. "Disturbing the peace doesn't have any exemptions in law." Tim's father had been an elder in a local church and had shown Tim that passage about shouting your religion from the streets. He had used it with two preachers before. One who read the passage and stopped the noise, one who didn't. Tim said the one who kept on didn't believe a word he was spouting. The passage warns that those who shout their religion from the streets shall not know the kingdom of heaven. Very plainly.

Tim wasn't religious to any extent. Neither he nor Clay could swallow what the organized churches (read businesses) were spouting, always in need of funds for their good works. O'Mally was one of those. He needed money to spread the word. He drove a brand spanking new BMW. That told Tim how devout he really was.

These were the bigger issues with the police in Seaview.

Tim and Clay were together at the hardware

store when the radio announced that Roberta Singer was at the station. There was a boat on fire off of Sandy Point. She had been to the fire department, who sent a boat out. They said to report it to the police. If they were needed they would be called. Clay and Tim headed for the office. Just as they arrived the police band came on to say a boat was going immediately. A policeman was needed on that boat because there was a body.

"We think it was a vent problem, that the boat exploded when the ignition was turned on, but the police have to be called when there's a death," Kyle Charles, fire chief, said. "We have the fire out and there is ... what? Give me a second ... there is? Clay, Dan says there's a bullet hole in the guy's head! It's that political hack ... whatever ... from Grandvista. Boars."

"Shit!" Clay cried.

"That covers it. Pick you up in two minutes. Got a coroner yet? I can call Doc Forbes."

"Forbes and Tim and I will come out. We can use Doc and you for our CSI team."

"Ten four."

"So he was shot in the chest, then in the head," Doc reported. "Either was fatal. I'd say a thirty eight, but we can maybe find the slugs somewhere. Kyle will have to sift whatever he can. All this fiberglass shouldn't make it too hard to find the slugs. It wasn't hot enough to melt lead, I don't think."

"I don't have a tiny clue as to where to start an investigation," Tim complained. "I'm damned glad it's Clay's headache."

"We saw him going out ... he stopped at the dock. They'll know if anyone else was aboard. If not, we have to know who *was* out there," Clay replied. "I doubt ... if there was someone aboard, we have to find where they got off."

They looked along the beach. A few people were not far. They had come out because of the fire. The tide was coming in, so they were retreating steadily up the beach.

This boat had stopped during the hottest part of the day. There wouldn't have been many, if any, on the beach at low tide. He could hope someone saw something. There weren't houses close here.

Sandy Point was a long spur that went out into the ocean for several hundred feet at low tide and wasn't a good place for swimming or such.

The closest houses were the Young's and the Reddings. He would check with them on the off chance someone was outside and had seen anything.

"Doc, can you tell if he was shot here? Was the boat fired immediately?"

Forbes studied his notes, then went to the body bag and opened it to study the corpse for a minute.

"Not likely."

"Then the boat was driven or pulled. Either case would mean another boat," Clay returned. "There's an outside chance someone saw it. Maybe someone heard a shot."

Doc nodded and zipped the body bag. He waved for them to put it on the fire department boat, said he had all he could find here and got on the boat, himself.

A fireman called that he had found a slug. Brass jacket forty. Probably a Glock was used.

Tim bagged the slug. They checked one more time, then headed for the office.

"What next?" Tim asked.

"You go to Grandvomit to ask around about him, his contacts, his enemies and all the standard stuff. I try to find anyone who saw the other boat."

Elena Redding was home, but didn't see or hear anything. She was in front of the house, mostly, so didn't see anything in back.

Anne Young was home. She was mostly in the house that time of day, so wouldn't see or hear anything because of the air conditioning. Her two children were playing back there. She called them. The 7 year old girl, Nika, said she saw a boat come to the other boat that got there at the same time and they all left but the boat was there that got all the smoke and stuff on it before the other boats came with the police and all that.

It was a white boat that looked like the white boat that got all the smoke and stuff except it was littler and had green where the other one had blue and didn't have a cabin that was the same kind and she didn't look out there much because sometimes there were a lot of boats but usually there wasn't anything when the sand was out of the water and it was just a boat and she wouldn't be able to see if it was the same one if they showed it to her. The one with all the smoke and stuff didn't have a motor on back like the other one. It had two or three and was pointed in front while the other one was more like a regular boat.

That was all Clay was able to get. Boars' boat was a 26 foot HarborCraft, so the other boat was smaller. A different cabin style probably meant it wasn't a HarborCraft. The other boat was outboard, the HarborCraft inboard. Pointed in front, two or three motors. A cigarette boat.

There wasn't any drug action in the water close to the area. That included Grandvista, which was a point in its favor. There could be some usage, but no traffic.

A cigarette boat would be easy to trace. Clay radioed Tim to find any cigarette boat in the area. Green trim or what have you.

"There are twenty five or thirty of them here. The High Seas Racing Club," Tim replied. "It's a status symbol to have a cigarette boat.

"Hey! Most of them are out of the water! I'll see which ones were in the storage. Maybe we can eliminate most of them."

Clay waited in the station for about an hour, then went to his apartment to fix a spaghetti dinner. Tim called that he was back. He had some news, but most of it was bad.

Clay went to the office to see what they could put together.

"A cigarette boat was stolen from the Whitewater Marina sometime after midnight and before four AM, when the crew came to work. Belonged to a Frederick Grossman. He's raising hell about it being stolen when there was a night watchman to see such things didn't happen. The watchman was in the little guardhouse. They couldn't wake him up. The hospital said he'd been drugged. It was a touchy thing. Too much. An overdose.

"Boars' platform was the corruption running rampant through the public offices, the court, the police, the commissioners, and the dogcatcher. He wasn't squeaky clean, according to several people I talked with, off the record.

"He was threatened by several people, but for lawsuits. Not bodily threats. He wasn't liked much, but was the type who people would figure they could use for connections. He was running for a position where he could make a few million a year from graft and bribes and so forth."

"I see. Sort of what I figured. He would be in a position to cut out a lot of people and rake it all off himself."

Tim aped shock. "Wha...? But he was running *against* corruption! He *promised*!"

"Yes. Is there any incidence where he actually kept a promise? Off the top of your head?"

Tim shook his head and grimaced. "Where does that leave us?"

"How many people in Grandvomit?"

"About three thousand."

"Well, that's our suspect list. We might as well get at it. It seems the murder is in our bailiwick. That means there's a ten or twelve percent chance we can solve it."

"Yeah. Compared to a tenth or twelfth percent chance there."

"Any special people we should concentrate on?"

"The people who want to build a casino and resort on that part in the north section of the town. They have state approval, but that depends on the individual town agreeing. It would have to be within the town limits, which means the mayor and council would have to approve it."

"So? He didn't win any election yet."

"But he was running on a platform that made him have to come out in opposition until the election. He was running ahead. It was making for bad publicity that he wouldn't be able to reverse if he won. He would have to wait a year or more before he could claim they had an agreement that was for the good of the town. The bad taste from the election would still be there. The bribes and so forth would be triple or quadruple or more."

"It could be, but I really don't think so. If we show they were involved in this kind of assassination they couldn't ever get final approval and their reputation would follow them anywhere. If you could get that information, someone else could get it – and use it. There's a thing or six that aren't fitting here."

"Well, it will have to wait for tomorrow. I'm tired."

They went home. As Tim said, it would have to wait for tomorrow.

Clay went to the office at nine to relieve Andy Lock, the night shift cop. Nothing of note had happened.

After checking out the regular things he went to the file they were gathering about Boars. Andy had taken some time on the computer to find what he could there. He had been to Guatemala and Honduras when he was seventeen and had been to Norway when he was twenty four. All trips were for less than a month.

There's something the opposition could have made some big waves about! Samuel Thomas Boars had been married when he was eighteen to a Wanda Madison. She had a child that had some characteristics that didn't fit with him, so he had a DNA match ordered. It wasn't his kid. He got a divorce. She didn't get anything.

Characteristics that didn't fit? What was that about?

He went to the computer and spent two hours searching what he could find. Nothing definite, but it could be that the kid was oriental or black.

He called Doc and told him about that case. Doc

said it might just make things a lot easier on him. He was also finding characteristics that didn't fit with the body.

"Such as?"

"The body had old broken bones and a bridge-work that, so far as I can find, Boars didn't."

"Is that ... but ... now it really doesn't make any sense!"

"Where was the DNA test made?"

"Jackson, Mississippi."

"I'll get back when I have an answer or two."

Clay sat back. He knew the methods of working the detective end of crimes, but murder was a bit out of his specialty. This one wasn't really his responsibility. He was sure he would be better off to call in the state.

Give it one more day.

There was a call about someone breaking into Chancy's Market. Cigarettes and a couple of very expensive watches were missing and a box that had several gross of condoms. The alarm had not sounded. The drugstore part wasn't entered. It had separate specialty security doors.

"The alarm was set and operative?" Clay asked George Chancy.

"Yeah. Brand new. It was tested first thing. It was on and working. I don't see how it was possible to not set it off. We had to re-regulate it two nights ago because a dog ran into the rear door. It was too sensitive.

"I mean, you could go to any door or window and just tap, you know, like you would knock on a door?"

"Where is it? The master panel."

George showed him a fancy box with a card slit and a keyboard.

"Double failsafe. You can turn it on or off with the card, but you have to type in the code at the same time."

There was a little sticker on the box that said, "Impenetrable Systems, Grandvista." He took the phone number and address.

"Some of those hoods from there know how to get around the system?" George asked. "I should know not to deal with those people, but this is the best system around here."

Clay looked around, thought a bit, and asked, "What can you show me about the watches that are missing?"

"Yeah. I got the pictures from the catalogue in case somebody tries to pawn them or like that." He showed the pictures. They were 18 karat gold bands with six diamonds around the face. Ladies watches. Retail price $1,249.95.

"Somebody wanted to ... I have to know who was involved in installing the system."

George went to his little office to search through a file cabinet of receipts. He handed Clay one.

"The installer was a woman?"

"Yeah. Not heavy work or anything. She knew her business. Why?"

"Because no one could get by this system except someone with a card and the code. Someone else could get the card or the code, but not both. The card would have to be copied, which very few can do, but the system can have several people with a card."

"Yeah. I got two. A backup. You can't use the same code with two cards. She could copy a card, but she wouldn't know the code."

Clay grinned.

"Why would she take the condoms? Wouldn't that say it was a guy?"

"It could also make us think it was a guy."

"But that's what ... oh!"

"I'll call state judge Carlyle to have him issue me a state investigation extension, then I'll go over there to arrest her."

"How did she do it?"

"She made three cards. You enter your own code that she wouldn't know. She just entered a code of her own on that third card."

"You can't trust nobody!"

"It's getting there. Shirley Ames. I doubt she can

get out of it."

"Yeah. I hope we can get the watches back. That's twenty five hundred bucks I'd have to spend another grand on to collect the insurance."

Clay went back to the office. Doc called a few minutes later to say the body, proven through DNA checks from the charts when the test was made on the baby, that the body was not Boars. It was not a close relative. There was one chance in thirty one thousand he was a relative not more removed than third cousin.

"Which brings up another question or ten thousand," Clay replied. "When was ... was that one the one who went out in the boat, or was that Boars? If it was Boars he doesn't have a chance in thirty one thousand of getting out of a murder one charge."

"You think maybe someone substituted somebody else for Boars ... but the people there knew him. It wouldn't work."

"I have to go over there. I'll get Boars' fingerprints. He was ... he had a passport for years. We can match what I can show were his to that passport."

"I don't follow, but go for it."

Tim came in. Clay said he had to pick up a state court order. He would be in Grandvomit the rest of the day.

"Don't try to play this game on me," Clay said to Shirley Ames. They were in the Impenetrable Systems office. "If you can show me any other way to get past the system without setting off the alarms, I'll listen."

"Well, that is, why would I take condoms? I mean ... oh, God! You didn't say anything about condoms.

"Look. I just wanted the watch. I saw it there and just had to have it. I never did anything like that before. I'll give it back and pay for the damned condoms or whatever. Don't put me in jail. I never did that before. I won't do anything like it again. I swear!"

"Well, you can't work in a security business anymore," the supervisor said. "It's up to the officer about the rest of it.

"You've been a good worker. I can try to get you work with my brother as a secretary. He doesn't have anywhere you could cause trouble."

"One thing," Clay said. "It was two watches."

She looked scared. "I swear! There was only one! Why would I want two! I swear!"

"So. George was going to run a little scam on the insurance," Clay said. "He doesn't deserve any consideration. Give me the watch and condoms and cigarettes and I'll drop charges."

"Cigarettes? There weren't any cigarettes.

They're in the drugstore and I didn't go in there. It might just be a story, but I think stealing tobacco or booze makes it federal. No way!"

"I see. So George is the real crook here. Maybe I can turn that back on him. It was another piece for the insurance bit. You took the watch and condoms. You'll return them and won't testify against him to the tobacco and alcohol board.

"This never happened. I think you've learned a lesson."

Clay arranged that. He was damned glad George lived in Wilthorn, six miles inland, not in Seaview. He then went to find what he could about Boars. He was given access to the house and environs where Boars had lived. He found an old passport in a file cabinet and a newer one. He took some things from the bathroom and kitchen. Doc could run DNA tests on them to determine who was living there.

He soon headed back to Seaview. He dropped the samples off for Doc, then went to the office. He and Tim went to Chancy's

Clay had the condoms and the watch in a box he put on George's desk. "We will have to wait for the alcohol and tobacco man before we handle this," Clay explained to George.

"ER!! Uh, that is ... alcohol and tobacco?"

"Yes. You made a report that two cases of

cigarettes were stolen. That makes it a federal felony. Two cartons could make that charge. We're talking about a hundred cartons. As you know from buying the things, that represents more than a thousand dollars in state and federal taxes. Naturally they want to authenticate the charge. That puts the thief in the federal pen for a minimum of four years."

George was sweating. "Er, I may have ... that is ... I mean, I found the cigarettes. I was going to call you. Louise put them in the drug store behind the counter and I thought they were still out here, you see."

"You charged that girl with a federal crime and didn't get around to reporting that it was a mistake?" Tim asked, aghast.

"I didn't charge her with that. There's no way she could have carried two cases of cigarettes out of there," Clay said. "Now. About the two watches. Do you have anything to say about that?"

George put his face in his hands. "I thought you would never catch anyone."

"So that makes it alright?"

"No. It makes me a shithead."

"We'll drop it all around. Try something like this again and I'll run you through a meat grinder. Got it?"

"I have, as you say, got it."

Clay and Tim got up and walked out. They went to the station to compare notes. Doc said the one on the slab hadn't been the one living in that house.

"First order of business now is to find out who is on that slab – and where Boars is," Clay suggested. Tim agreed.

"We know one thing for sure. He wasn't from around here," Doc said. "No one from around here is missing. We would have noticed a stranger who looks that much like the erstwhile Mr. Boars."

Tim said, "We can send an internet request for a missing person who fits the DB. That will be fastest – if he's from anywhere near here."

"I think he was probably being used in some scheme for some time," Clay suggested. "Something happened to make someone else change the plan.

"Tim, you and Doc try to find who he was. I'm going to be looking for Boars. If I find him we get the answers to most of it. He'll spill. He doesn't have a chance of getting out of a murder one rap with this one. I'll be most interested in his story. It will be a good one."

"With holes you could drive a sixty five footer through," Doc replied. "Politicians. They think people will actually believe the shit they spout.

"A little connecting point here. The slug came from a Glock forty owned by someone named, what was it? Sam Something. Boars? I think that was it.

"Seems he shot the guy with a registered gun. Rather stupid, wouldn't you say?"

"I'd say something a lot like that," Tim agreed. Clay looked thoughtful, then smirked.

"He's about half as smart as he thinks he is," Clay said.

"Who? Boars?" from Doc.

"Among others. I think the best laid plans of politicians and thugs can sometimes go awry!"

That got him a couple of one finger salutes and a couple of questioning grins.

Clay headed for the computer. It seemed a lot of police work was handled that way anymore. It was faster and more complete than the old legwork methods. He also wanted to be there when one of three possible calls came in. It was about the right time. The newspapers had some pictures and questions printed this morning, so the calls would start coming. Which came first might tell a story by simply that sequence.

Oakvale. That was a little town one mile inland and six miles along the coast. Boars had worked for a trucking company there five and a half until four years ago, when he moved to Grandvista to immediately become involved in politics. A job with the zoning board as inspector. He would know people in Oakvale.

He got an idea. He checked out that trucking company. JKLMT Movers and Haulers.

Statewide. Had several big garbage disposal companies as subsidiaries. Had two road builder subs. President and CEO, Gino Chatters – suspected mob boss.

Mobs and politics. About what he expected.

Janet called from in front to say there was a call for the officer in charge of the murder investigation department. There was a giggle in her voice. Like they had departments for each kind of crime with just four officers?

He picked up the phone. "Fordham. Violent Crimes. Can I help you?"

"I am Theresa Simpkins. I am in Lambton. My husband is missing since yesterday morning. He is involved with some very scary people. I think they are gangsters. He looks like the picture of the missing man. S. T. Boars. There was a body on a burnt boat that was supposed to be Boars, but wasn't."

Lambton was another very small town about fifteen miles away, past Oakvale and more inland.

"What is your husband's full name? What kind of work did he do?"

"William George Simpkins. He is a dispatcher at Miller's Movers."

Clay quickly brought Miller's Movers to screen. It was a subsidiary of Carter Carriers, a subsidiary of JKLMT.

"Is there a way we can definitely identify him? A birthmark or scar or old broken bone?"

"Well, he had some dental work. He had two broken ribs three years ago. Left side. Let's see. He had a scar on his left arm. Maybe three inches long. Not very obvious, but you could see it."

"The dental work. A bridge?"

"Yes. Three teeth on the lower left side."

"Do you know his dentist?"

"I think he used Dr. Peterson in Oakvale. I'm not too sure."

"We can check it out. I hate to say something like this on a telephone, but prepare yourself for some very bad news. We can hope it's not ... do you understand?"

"I wish I didn't."

He turned her over to Janet and called Doc. "Three teeth on the lower left?"

"Who?"

William George Simpkins, Lambton. Dr. Peterson, Oakvale for confirmation. Also two broken ribs, left side."

"It'll be him. Connection?"

"Political. Dispatcher for truckers. Subs of JKLMT. Garbage and road construction contractors.”

“Chatters. This could get nasty. Even more than now. I’m on it.”

Getting that call first would confuse what he was thinking.

Maybe not. If it was done that way it could be deliberately. To cause confusion.

“Clay! Boars!” Janet called.

Clay picked up the phone.

“Yes?”

“You’re Officer Fordham?”

“Yes.”

“I’m outside of Luke Wang Chinese, on the side behind where the cardboard boxes are stored. I think there’s someone trying to kill me. Other than that man who looked a little too much like me who tried to kill me on my boat. I’m the one who shot him. It was at a private dock at the big sandstone place in Oakvale Coast. The fancy teak dock. I ran down the beach and came here. I stayed in the barn at the milk farm on Riser Road. Two men came by four times during the night, very slow, in a car.

“I crossed some very powerful people. I’m running for mayor in Grandvista. I think some kind of mob is after me to stop me. Please don’t let anyone know about this call. They might have someone right there in your department who would tell them where to find me."

"Okay. Half an hour, max. If I rush out after getting a call it could arouse suspicion, so I'll finish this report, then leave like I'm going on patrol."

"Good thinking!"

Also, I want to wait for the next call, that should come within fifteen minutes.

He sat back to think. The call came three minutes later. He picked up the phone before Janet got it.

"Fordham. Police. How can I serve you?"

"I'm just ... officer, I saw that Boars man, I'm sure. He was coming from the beach to the road. The road to Oakvale. It was about five o'clock yesterday afternoon. I just saw the thing in the paper a minute ago and felt I should tell someone."

"Thank you. It should help establish a timeline.

"Your name?"

"Oh ... A murdered man? I won't give you my name. I did my duty. I don't want to be the next one found dead in a boat!" She hung up.

Clay grinned.. Boars admitted the killing. It was a matter of it being self-defense or murder one.

That meant finding if there was a motive. He could think of one really big one right now.

Trouble being it was one really big one for two

very different people. If he got the wrong one it could screw up a lot of things and cause a lot of grief to a lot of people.

He would talk with Boars. There was no way he would get away with anything now.

He also wanted to talk with the other candidates for mayor of Grandvista. He didn't follow the elections there, but couldn't help but hear about some things. There was also the cop gossip that he wasn't into, but it was possible Tim listened to some of it. A cop could get some useful information there, it was a matter of being able to separate facts from fantasies.

He called Tim. They took a couple minutes to make a plan. They needed something that would throw one hell of a scare into several people. It would be a matter of making the ones who thought they were in control wonder if maybe there was another rat in that woodpile.

"I'm going to look like I'm going on patrol," he told Janet. "If anyone asks that's all you know."

"Okay."

He strolled out and went toward the Oakvale road, to Luke Wang's Chinese.

"I wasn't followed. Nobody paid any attention to me. I made it a point to be noticed, which I wouldn't do if I was doing what I'm doing."

"You're intelligent. Good!" Boars replied. "I'm in the middle of one hell of a mess. I shouldn't have come down so hard on certain people until I have the means to thwart their schemes.

"You know I'm running for mayor. I plan to build that into running for the senate in a few years. They need people who aren't owned by the crime syndicates – and we do have them, even here in little Lower Podunk.

"I'd heard for the past couple of years that there was a man who looked almost like my twin in the area. It didn't register as anything special. We all have people who resemble us somewhere.

"When I stopped at that dock and saw him coming out it was like a mirror!

"I didn't think much of that. It could be a joke Paul Anderson was playing. He does things like that and it's his house.

"Then he had a pistol all of a sudden! He was aiming right at me!

"I ducked below the console and got my own from there. It's this one. He shot and missed me half an inch, so I shot him. Twice, I think. He dropped right there on the dock and someone was coming from the house. I don't know who he was, but he had a rifle.

"There's a little ramp under the dock to the beach. I knew I wouldn't have a chance against a rifle on the water so I jumped out and ran up the ramp to the wall and along the wall, low, until I was around the bend.

"I got to the road and ran along it a ways, then thought that was stupid. They would get a car and shoot me like a pigeon!

"I went off the road and through the brush along there to just outside of town at the milk farm. I could hear and see cars along the road all the way. I could hide when they passed. A black BMW went by several times, slow. I think it went by the milk farm four times after dark.

"I came here and called you. You have a rep that says you can't be bought or intimidated and won't back down from God.

"Here we are."

After not calling last night or as soon as you got off the beach? Why wait until nine thirty to call?

"I see. The main one you would have to consider with choosing your platform would have to be

Chatters. This is a bit blatant, even for a crud like him."

"I don't think it's him. He's made it clear, personally, that he thinks he's above what I could hope to do as mayor."

"I have to consider a lot of things. One is that Simpkins worked for a subsidiary of a subsidiary of JKLMT. That's Chatters all the way."

"Simpkins?"

"The DB. Dispatcher for one of Chatter's companies."

For the first time Boars looked actually scared.

Little surprise there! He actually tried to shoot you! Why the change of plans?

"I can try to find a safe place for you. Maybe Tim will know a way. We have to get this investigation moving. It won't be good for the election for you to not be available. Nobody would vote for you."

"If you can convince whoever is trying to kill me that it would only make it plain who they are maybe I can get back ... I can have police protection under the circumstances in Grandvista. Maybe you could arrange that and get me there, then it wouldn't be your problem anymore. I can hint I left a lot of material with you. Your rep would guarantee they wouldn't touch me."

"Only if you know which one or ones are behind

it. You sort of let Chatters off the hook."

My-my! Don't you look confused now! Is it because you had a deal or because Chatters isn't keeping his end?

"Well, I'm sure they won't try anything if I'm with you, so we can go somewhere. We can try to sort it out."

"Okay. Let's head for the office. I can call Tim in from patrol and he can arrange something."

They went out to the street and were just past the old abandoned block ice building when there was a shot that missed Boars' head by inches. Clay dragged him down and drew his service Glock, but there was no one to be seen. The shot, by the sound, had come from across the street. There were a lot of thick shrubs and such over there.

Clay radioed that he and a citizen were under fire and gave the location. He kept Boars down on the sidewalk with him between the field and Boars. Tim came running up with a riot gun less than two minutes later. Clay pointed to the shrubbery. Tim went carefully into the lot, then came back to call that no one was there, but a shell casing from a .30-.30 was.

Clay told Boars to stay very low and they went on to the office. Boars would give a statement to Janet, then they would get him to Grandvista.

Tim and Clay went to the seaside porch to

discuss the case.

"Scare him enough?" Tim asked.

"He's almost convinced. I'm damned glad you're a trained sniper! That shot didn't miss him more than two inches. It was perfect! He was almost against that wall. No one could doubt the shot was meant for him. The powder from the concrete where the slug hit popped right onto his face.

"I think it'll make more than just Boars and Chatters damned nervous. There's someone they neither one know anything about involved."

"There couldn't be anyone. Chatters' network is too tight for that."

"So he used to think!"

They did a high five.

They discussed the next step, which was getting Boars back to Grandvista where he would become their responsibility. By now he would doubt everyone of them. He knew they were corrupt. That meant anyone with the money could buy them.

"What will they do now?" Tim asked. "They'll have to draw back to figure who's about to make a big power play. Anything this blatant means whoever it is has something."

"Now we have to wait to see what their next move will be. I think this was just to make Boars a shoo-in for mayor, so we have to know what's planned other than that casino. Someplace where the mayor can make a difference. I can't figure where the next thing will come from, but they've made a huge mistake to get us involved. I think they'll be getting a glimmer about now.

"I also think ... that I don't have a clear picture of what happened at that dock. It was probably set up in Boars' mind that he would thwart an attempt to kill him, but the guy was shooting real bullets.

"If Boars knew ... that there was to be a phony attack ... he is guilty of murder one. He fully meant to kill Simpkins.

"I wonder why the look-alike was used. It doesn't make sense. Was Chatters pulling a doublecross, or was Boars, or were they both ... which means that there really is someone else."

Tim nodded. Janet called that the statement was ready. Clay could be one witness to the signing, but they had to have someone totally uninvolved for the other.

Gus Gormann was walking by. Clay asked him to witness. They handled that, then Clay said Tim would be in charge until he returned. He was taking a citizen in danger to Grandvista.

They headed for Grandvista. Clay chatted about things in general, but got no hints from Boars.

Boars really was scared, so maybe it really was a doublecross by Chatters.

Why would he do that?

Clay hid his grin. So! It was still a conspiracy murder involving Chatters and Boars, but there was someone else in that game Boars didn't know.

Chatters probably had this planned for a long time. He had his own plans for the political end.

Boars was delivered. Clay said he would use the time he was in Grandvista anyhow to take care of a few things.

He wanted to interview the other two candidates for mayor. He called and was told Johnson would be available after four. Pantry had fifteen minutes or so now.

"Mr. Pantry? I'm Clay Fordham, cop from Seaview. I have a few questions if you will be so kind?"

"Of course! I intend to eliminate Boars at the voting booth, not before – and certainly not in any such matter. Bringing out a few truths about him will handle that quite well, I think. He has some very unsavory connections, you know. Connections with the very people he claims to be going after if elected."

"Chatters et al. I know. I think his connections with those types already has him wondering if he's ten percent as smart as he thought he was. I think he had it set up to have an attempt made on his life he could point to as proof he was actually going after them. Something went radically wrong. He killed the one who was supposed to be charged with attacking him. I can't help but wonder why he...! I'll be damned! He as much as told me, but doesn't know it.

"Okay. Straight out. Are you the one who Chatters is setting up to win this election?"

"No. I have had offers."

"You won't say who. That's understandable."

"Yes. The police would know how it works. I have a family. I won't accept their offer, but I won't say anything about it to anyone who may give it publicity."

"Do you know Paul Anderson?"

"The name sounds familiar. I don't know any such person more than having heard the name."

"Politics here are very different from Seaview. I have a different situation in a lot of ways. I can't let this kind of thing get a foothold there. Our mayor runs unopposed. We don't have any major crime issues."

"Yes. You also have people who are very wealthy and very solvent. We have people who wish for you to think they're wealthy. They are most often in debt to an extent they can't realistically hope to earn enough in their lifetimes to rise above. Your people are savvy about the schemes to get their wealth and turn such affairs over to people with expertise in avoiding financial problems. These people are the ones with the schemes. Too often, criminal schemes."

"You do see the problem. If you eliminate the corruption, you automatically eliminate most of your problems."

Panty nodded and grimaced. "We try. It's an uphill fight all the way. Those people are there and determined to stay there. Some of us are determined to get them out, but they have the advantage."

They chatted a few minutes more, then Clay headed for a lunch and to talk with people at the political headquarters. He learned that every one of them made claims about the others being too close to the mob bosses. Until the people got so sick of it they got together to get rid of all of them nothing was going to change. The people in Grandvista didn't have the spine to hold together long enough to dump the crooks. The people in the headquarters were often really intent on doing something, but they couldn't find a candidate who could deliver anything at all. Even if they elected a mayor who meant what he promised, the council would overturn anything he did.

Every area headquarters had a councilman or two they were promoting. Clay forbore asking why they griped about the council overturning the mayor when they were also elected officials promoted by the same headquarters. It was a matter of getting *all* of them out.

"We can't get an honest person to accept the job," and a shrug.

This was pathetic.

He went to Johnson's main headquarters at four. Johnson could spare a few minutes. It was hectic this close to election.

"Just a few things. It's about the attempt on Boars' life."

"Publicity stunt. Bullshit."

"There's a body."

"That Boars created for you. In self-defense? Then he runs and doesn't even call you for hours? Really?"

"We all have some hard questions about that. I was with him when another attempt was made."

"I heard something about that. Maybe someone did grab an opportunity to try to get him off the slate. It wasn't me."

"That was after ... do you know Paul Anderson?"

"I've heard of him. I can't say that...."

"Oh! That's right. You went to his place a couple of times a few weeks ago. I can't get the ... it's complicated, but I think deliberately."

"Er, yes. Paul. Out past you toward Oakvale? Yes. We had some meetings at his place. He's a big wheel in another party."

Bingo! I should have pulled that one with Pantry! That shook this one!

"He's tied up with politics everywhere except where he lives, it seems. His place is where Boars shot Simpkins.

"Chatters try to buy you yet?"

"He tries to buy everyone from the local street sweeper to the governor. He isn't always successful. I told him to take a walk. I'm not that dirty and don't ever intend to be. I've made mistakes, but not anything nearly on that order."

"Well, thanks. I'd better get back to my own bailiwick. We might have had something as serious as a kid shoplifting a candy bar while I was gone."

"While we had a few muggings and a murder or two, plus some hijackings and bank robberies."

"It seems that way at times."

They shook hands and left.

So. Paul Anderson was in a little deeper than just a house with a dock.

He thought for a minute, then went to Boars' headquarters. He was in back, staying out of sight and away from where anyone might be hurt if anything happened.

"Just wanted to ask one more thing. Tell me about Paul Anderson. He seems to be a meeting place for politicians from all the parties."

"He writes books and newspaper articles about politics. We meet at his place to debate and so forth. Sometimes we meet there to explain our policies."

"I heard Chatters and Shackles attend some of those meetings."

"Shackles? That gangster from the capital? I had heard he was there once, but no one could say for sure. Or would."

Clay nodded and waved, then headed back to Seaview. It seemed the mobs were on both sides of his town. That made it his business. He was in a position to be squeezed. Get either side of the squeeze out of the race and they couldn't put on much pressure. The one thing Seaview had was people with the ability and means to put on a lot more pressure from different directions than the crooks could.

He wanted to meet Anderson to have a little chat. He'd met him on the streets to say hello, but that was all. He wanted to know just how deeply Anderson was involved. He also wanted a couple of questions that were there all along answered.

"Well, Tim! The place is still here, I see. Any major crimes while I was gone?"

"Those Berman kids were in the Forbes' garden again. It seems we could do something to make those people keep their brats home."

"Solution?"

"Don't put the slide and such out there in an unfenced place that looks like a public park *because* of the slides and such so there won't be an implied permission. Other than that, fence the place in. They could post signs, but these were children who probably couldn't read them.

"Learn anything?"

"Other than that Paul Anderson might be in this a lot deeper than we thought and that everyone believes Boars was just pulling a publicity stunt and probably didn't even know the gun was loaded with real bullets.

"Oh, yeah. There's a rumor that Shackles was at Anderson's. Just a rumor."

"Shackles? So what? Anderson and even Chatters are so far below his league they can't see daylight."

"Which begs the question of what he was doing there, in that case. I just dropped his name because of how he got started in the garbage business. now Chatters is following in his footsteps."

"He's lagging a few miles behind. Shackles has that sewed tight in any area where it really counts."

Clay nodded. He went to his office and filed what he had, then went over the statement by Boars. He'd repeated it to Janet.

Doc came in. He hadn't learned anything more.

"Do you know Paul Anderson?"

"Slightly. He's tied into politics, but not that side."

"Yes. That side."

Doc raised an eyebrow.

"All the politicians in the area meet at his place to discuss political things. All parties."

Doc looked thoughtful. "Could be!"

"So I'll want to have a little chat with him tomorrow. About election strategies."

"Like how it would help Boars to have shot Simpkins instead of just scaring him off?"

"Among other things."

<u>*Chatting with Anderson*</u>

"Paul Anderson? I'm Clay Fordham."

"Come on in. I was expecting you yesterday."

"I had to spend yesterday in Grandvomit. I mean Grandvista."

"You had it right first time. I wasn't here when Boars came."

"I didn't ask. We knew that. It doesn't mean anything. Someone was. They put the body in the boat, took it to Sandy Point, fired it and left."

"I don't see...?"

"It was a setup. I don't think anyone was supposed to be killed. I think what was probably meant to be a joke backfired on you. You got that lookalike to come out there, it shook Boars up, the idiot fired a shot close to Boars, so Boars fired back and ran. You had a body on your hands so you put it in the boat and ran it to Sandy Point to fire it.

"You had people here. You had another boat here. A stolen boat, which was probably supposed to be seen running back to Grandvista to fix the story Boars would tell. What happened meant it told a far different story.

"Shackles behind it or just Chatters?"

"Chatters. We couldn't touch Shackles and know it."

"We?"

Anderson went to a safe to get some papers. Anderson was a state marshal working with a federal anticorruption unit.

"Give me a damned break! That bunch is just as corrupt as the ones they catch! They're a joke! Everyone in the country knows they only catch the ones who won't pay them off!"

Anderson grinned. "See? You ain't got no problem with those jerk-offs. Let's make a deal."

"No kidding? They cultivate that image?"

"Uh-huh. Shackles thinks he's bought off enough that he can throw us the competition. We'll handle it for him."

"He's throwing you Chatters?"

"The population's grown enough in the area that he can make a profit on the garbage and such.

"Chatters set up Boars. This was to guarantee he'd get ninety nine percent of the vote. Big public hero. Chatters doesn't have the control he wants on Boars. Boars will hold him up for millions and will get his hands into the casino people – who aren't what he thinks, either.

"Chatters may have sent Simpkins as a joke, but he's not the joking type. I don't get that part. The plan seems to keep changing. All I heard was that something about the time of the report being too much. I don't know what it's about."

"Depends on which time. Boars above a little blackmail?"

"He's not above anything."

Clay started laughing. Anderson asked why.

"Way I see it. Boars was supposed to run off someone who threatened him. The wrong person was there to make the supposed threat – not as a joke, but to make Boars see they have someone who can do things to end his career. Have him meet with all the wrong people at the wrong time and get pictures. From even a little distance no one could tell it wasn't Boars. They probably already have a set of pictures for just that. Boars was going to put the screws to Chatters, Chatters had a counter that would guarantee he wouldn't get elected to street sweeper.

"I'd be willing to bet Simpkins didn't have any gun when he went out there. He probably had a few pictures. Boars lost it and shot the messenger.

"Now he's in real and immediate trouble. He's got a dead body on his hands. He calls friends from Grandvista to come in that cigarette boat and take care of things. One of them fires a couple of shots into the boat to make it look like Boars was being shot at.

"Boars is thinking as fast as he can manage. It would be logical that he would run. He could use the excuse of someone with a rifle, so it couldn't be by water.

"He went to the road, being sure he was seen there, then went somewhere else for the night to set up his stage.

"The too much time was because he called me at nine in the morning, not immediately from where he was supposedly shot at. I was suspicious as hell about that all along.

"I set up the shot at him in Seaview. That threw a curve to both him and Chatters ... I'll bet he called Chatters when he shot Simpkins! He was going to put the screws to him right then and there! Someone shooting at Boars in Seaview they didn't have a hint about? Was there someone else trying to take over something?

"So Boars is now in hiding in public. Chatters doesn't dare do anything there. Boars has something to tag Chatters, Chatters can ruin Boars. Mexican standoff – but who else is involved?

"Does Chatters know anything about Shackles wanting to take him over?"

"I think he has a hint, but nothing definite. He'll think Shackles is behind it and wants Boars out of the picture so he can go after Chatters. Neat!"

"We have to find a way to use it. I have an idea.

Boars made one other huge mistake. I think he knows it by now."

"Mistake?"

"He hinted to me that he had told Chatters he left some things with me in case anything unpleasant happened to him. That means he has something.

"Chatters has that monstrosity of a place in toward the lake, doesn't he?"

"The whole side of the lake. Eight hundred acres."

"Maybe I'll go calling. Can you get in touch with him?"

"Uh-huh. You have something in a safe place. I don't know what it is or where it came from, but it can put his ass in the pen for at least fifteen to twenty. Do *not* cross you!

"It's still dangerous as hell. Don't take any chances where he's concerned."

"I never planned to live forever. Something else occurs to me."

"What?"

"If you were Shackles and decided to come after Chatters, would you use some dink of a politician and schemes or would you just come in and take over? Consider what we know Shackles is."

"Meaning Chatters has a little thing or two himself. Very possible."

"Is Shackles about through for your purposes?"

"Yeah. Might as well see if we can take him out without it looking like we had anything to do with it. Some hick cop found something, some hillbilly with morals and all that kind of obsolete thing. He took the big bad mafia don down. What a man's supposed to do when confronted with a crook!"

They shook hands. This could well get interesting now.

Good Evening, Mr. Chatters

Clay pulled up to the gate to Chatters' place by Lake Heron. He told the guard there he was Clay Fordham and would like to speak with Mr. Chatters about a thing or two. They seemed to expect him and passed him through.

He parked in a space by the house entrance and sauntered to the door, where an obvious goon was waiting. The goon asked if he was carrying. He said just the one in the holster on his belt. He wasn't about to start anything when he was outgunned fifty to one.

The goon grinned and waved him in. He went through a large room with curved marble staircases to either side and into a hall paneled with rare teak, then into a smaller room where another goon looked at the pistol, shrugged and waved them through.

Chatters was a slightly fat ugly man with thick black (obviously dyed) hair. He was sitting behind a huge mahogany desk and pointed the Cuban cigar he was smoking at a comfortable chair. He told the goon to bring him a Scotch on the rocks and Mr. Fordham whatever he wanted.

Clay said coffee if they had any made.

"Colombian? Panamanian? Arabian?"

"Whatever. I'm a coffee addict."

"Sugar and cream?"

"Black. If it's strong, one sugar. On the side. I probably won't use it."

The goon went to the bar to pour the Scotch, brought it to Chatters and went out.

"Well, Mr. Fordham. Paul called and informed me you were holding some things Mr. Boars gave you?"

"No. I didn't say Boars or anyone else gave it to me."

He laughed. "Can't catch you that easy. What did you want to say?"

"I really want to ask a few questions about the recent incident with Simpkins.

"Do you think it was smart to send Simpkins out there first?"

"No. That was a stupid thing to do. I should have sent Niko or Franko. I wanted shock value, but not to the extent it happened."

The goon brought a large mug of rich-smelling coffee. He said, "Panamanian. Julia had it perked already."

Clay tasted it and nodded his approval. It was rich and delicious. Chatters told the goon this was a private conversation about business. See they weren't disturbed. The goon left.

"You see, Paul said you figured it for very close to what it was. I find him useful, he thinks he's using me. C'est la vie."

"Yes. I like Paul. He's got sense enough to stay out of my way, in a manner of speaking, so I stay out of his whenever possible.

"You said that Boars might have given me something. That was something that, under some circumstances, you shouldn't have said. It tells me Boars has something. It tells me that, seeing he's the kind to bring up such things, he might have something about someone else. It could put both of you in a very bad position. You can be glad whoever it is didn't hit him. I imagine he's considered it by now and has come to the same conclusion. If that weren't the case there would have been another attempt. Perhaps a successful one. Perhaps I would be here with a SWAT team for another reason altogether."

"Oh? You think you could prove any of it?"

"I work on combinations, not one direction. A piece here that fits a piece there and I have something solid when following only one thing would leave me with suspicions I couldn't, as you suggested, prove."

"You tend to be as up-front as your reputation. For that reason I can't understand why you're here."

"To stop this crap from coming to Seaview. Paul understands that he must keep things away. I want you to understand that it applies to you. There's one hell of a lot of money in Seaview, not a hell of a lot of debts. Those people don't bother anyone. Don't bother them."

"I have my garbage service there. I don't go past what is, on its face, legal. The pickup is legal. Why and how I got that contract is possibly questionable. C'est la vie."

"I also want to give a word that you may be aware of. Beware of anyone by the name of Shackles. I feel he is behind something ... that he has shown ... let's say, he has designs. I'd much rather have you here than him."

"I see. There are rumors, but they are always there."

"Is Boars stupid enough to think he can blackmail someone like Shackles?"

"That might be a very possible scenario. Boars isn't the brightest star in the galaxy."

"I have to find who Shackles has here. I do *not* want them here! I have to find a way to stop him!"

"Yes. It becomes also urgent for my own needs. I will try to ascertain who it might be. If you will agree that we may trade information that is to our mutual advantage?"

"Yes. I will agree to trade information that is to mutual advantage. In a heartbeat!"

Chatters stood and offered his hand. Clay shook it.

To our MUTUAL advantage.

Clay headed back to Seaview. Tomorrow he would have a few things to discuss with Boars. He wanted to establish that Boars did have information about Chatters. He'd done that.

Who did Shackles have here? He would be trying to set that person up to handle things when he took over. There should be a trail.

He thought of another conversation. It very well could be. It would fit.

Maybe a little investigation of another matter.

Did Boars really have anything he thought could hold Chatters back? Would he be so stupid he would try to blackmail Shackles?

The drive back to Seaview at sunset was rather refreshing and calming. He hoped tomorrow would be as tranquil – but damned well doubted it.

"Paul, Johnson knew a little too much about what was going on. He's the one person who's in a position to get information he can pass on. He's just flippant enough that I know something's being put in place that should make him a long-shot winner. I think that's already decided. You know who has to be behind it.

"We have to consider that it will get rid of some corrupt snakes we want to be rid of. Trouble is, it will put an even more powerful snake in position to run things.."

"Shackles is a bit more savvy and pragmatic than the others. Pantry is the only honest candidate, but he hasn't got a smell of a chance. If he won it would get away from him the first week and they'd have a field day.

"We can't control it. We don't have a lever against anyone but Boars."

"You know that and I know that. None of them do. Even Shackles has to be wondering who fired that shot at Boars in Seaview. He has to be going crazy trying to find who was here who could have done it.

"He hasn't made any overt moves. That tells me Boars does have something. It also tells me it's not as strong as Boars thinks. Johnson is to be elected, so he's going to wait until just before the election to do something that will force Boars to react, then whatever he has will be something ... I'll be damned!"

"We probably both will. What?"

"Simpkins! I felt he went out there with pictures

that would show Boars with the wrong people! That's exactly what he did! Shackles was one of them, so Boars was going to use that. He would come out just before the election and claim something about the pictures, which would enhance his public image.

"They would have to be just pictures of him and Shackles. Maybe something to suggest a date or place.

"I know what Shackles plans! It doesn't have anything to do with Chatters. He's just a silly little puppet who can be a diversion. The pictures will be used to discredit Boars and him, leaving Shackles with Pantry, who he would walk over in a day, and his own candidate."

Anderson thought for a minute, then grinned. "This is going exactly to plan. We just didn't know which one's plan it was. Now we do.

"What do you suggest?"

"Why, this will have to be handled with a press conference the day before the election. They can all.... The debate the night before the election! That is going to turn into one grand melee! I promise!

"I studied a lot of pictures of Boars and a few of Simpkins. Tim got them from the widow. She took hundreds. I spotted something."

They put their heads together and came up with

a bit of a plan of their own. It's success would depend on Clay getting his hands on those photos. He had a lever.

In the morning he drove out to Chatters' place. Chatters wasn't exactly pleased to receive callers at seven thirty in the morning, but Clay had announced to the gateman that he wanted to discuss material held by various people. It was definitely to Chatters' advantage that such matters were discussed in private, not on a public forum.

He was passed through.

Chatters was on the terrace having breakfast. Clay would have a mug of gourmet coffee.

"I'll be blunt. I need copies of the pictures. There are some things you don't know that will slap you in the teeth tomorrow night."

"Pictures? I don't know what the hell you're talking about."

"The ones Simpkins was murdered over. There's someone – other than Boars – who has copies. You trusted the wrong person. He scanned them and sent them to another before he went out on that dock."

"It isn't you. You wouldn't want copies if you had them. Boars has a set. I have a set. I can't think of anyone else who would have any use for ... Johnson? Pantry?"

"You could laugh them off. You're way down

on the ladder with them."

"Simpkins didn't know anybody who ... did he?"

"Who owns fifty Simpkins in every county in this state? Who would be kept abreast of such things as a matter of course? Are you that blind?"

"So. What do you want with the pictures?"

"Such things have weight for a few days, like through election day, then they are authenticated or declared phony. Those pictures will be easy to prove false."

"Oh? How? I assure you that experts have already declared they're authentic."

"Then we can easily prove they're staged.

"It's to your advantage. Take the deal or leave it, but you're putting your neck on the block."

He looked thoughtful, shook his head, looked thoughtful again, and called Gino to bring him the file marked *Future Dump Sites - Oakvale* from his office.

The goon brought a thick manila envelope, dropped it on the table and left. Chatters shoved toward Clay, who looked through the pictures, grinned a few times and looked very surprised a couple of times.

"Okay. I'll take the wind out of their sails with these. I need copies of a few."

"I got two or three more sets in other places. Those are yours. If Shackles has it set up to win they ain't much good to me. Boars tries anything stupid, like he will, he's history in a lot of ways. I won't have to do it."

Clay said they agreed to exchange material that was to mutual advantage. This was.

He headed for the office. He called Paul to meet him there. And Tim.

<u>*A Hell of a Debate*</u>

"Gentlemen, we will try to act like gentlemen here," Anna Sherkov, moderator, declared. "Leave the dirty politics outside. We will debate issues on their merits, not on buzz words and propaganda.

"You have drawn numbers that will establish the order of answers. The questions were taken from a polling of the voting public. The first to answer will be number one on the first question, number two on the second, number three on the third and so forth.

"Confine your replies to the questions asked. Do not go into tangential subjects or you will be cut off.

"First question, number one, Mr. Pantry. You have two minutes to answer before it passes to the next candidate.

"How will you try to stabilize the confusing property tax structure we who live in Grandvista must endure?"

"The tax laws are a piecemeal conglomeration of poorly thought-out theories. I propose an entire new set of laws that treat equally the ...."

"... to see that such issues are dealt with immediately and finally," Boars finished nine questions later.

"Number three, Mr. Johnson: How do you propose to fight the corruption in the city and county government that is making Grandvista a joke to the rest of the state?"

"Why, by using an old tried and true method of exposing exactly who are the corrupt and who are the corruptors. I have here a set of photographs taken of Mr. Boars with Mr. Chatters, who is long suspected of corrupt practices and is presently under investigation by the state. I even have two of Mr. Boars with Mr. Shackles, who is under investigation both by the state and the federal government.

"Statements in places such as this that one is sworn to fighting corruption when that candidate is shown, positively, to be in contact with exactly those people can be exposed as easily as this! It also exposes a few things about Mr. Chatters and who he is or is not involved with for whatever purpose.

"I will allow Mr. Boars the rest of my time to reply?"

"You lousy goddamned slimy snake!" Boars screeched.

"Who? *Me?*"

Clay and Tim were to one side. They came onto the stage to hand Sherkov a couple of warrants.

"My god! This is a warrant for conspiracy murder against Boars and persons to be named later!" she cried. She looked at the second sheet. "And this is for on-the-spot authentication of photographs presented. An expert is here for that purpose.

"Well, people! This is a strange turn of events!"

Arnold Patterson, a state expert, came onto the stage. He announced that he had studied the photographs and declared they are phony. He was here merely to ascertain that the photographs here presented are identical copies of the ones he studied.

He took the photos from Johnson, looked at them carefully for about three minutes, then said they are the same.

"I will explain shortly. The photos are, themselves, authentic, in that they are photographs of persons here and not present. The falsity is in declaring that Mr. Boars is the same person shown in those photographs. He is not. The notched left ear and the scar on the left had do not appear on the person of Mr. Boars. These are photographs of a Mr. Simpkins, now deceased, appearing with these personages. There is some question that the two with a Mr. Shackles are computer overlays. It appears that they are.

"This suggests, though I am no expert in that area, that all but those two are what we called staged photographs, thus the other subjects were quite obviously aware the pictures were being taken. Whether this indicates fraud or more serious charges I am not qualified to state."

"What does that have to do with me being charged with conspiracy murder!?" Boars cried.

"On photographs seven nine and eleven there appears, first, an index fingerprint. On eleven there is a middle fingerprint. Those prints were on the lens and caused a very slight blurring of the photographs that could be brought out with pixel enhancement. They are your fingerprints, Mr. Boars. You were handling that camera when the photographs were taken or they would appear in all photos or none," Patterson replied. "Officer Fordham has declared that Simpkins was shot by you by your own admission. He was shot because he could show you were the photographer."

Boars simply stood and stared at the podium in front of him.

"You and Chatters very definitely were there. This was an election trick," Tim said. "You would declare the photos false and maneuver Clay into proving it. You knew very damned well that it would be easy to show it wasn't you in the pictures. It could be shown right here, like it was. You would walk away with the election.

"You left fingerprints, Mr. Boars. There's no other way they can be explained. You're going down!"

"I did not know about any of this!" Johnson yelled.

"Whatever. The debate is hereby closed," Sherkov said.

A few minutes later the stage was empty. "However you look at it, Shackles won this election," Clay said with a sour expression. "Johnson directly or Pantry indirectly. It's one hell of a long way from solving anything about corruption here, that's for damned sure!"

"It turned out to be, as you promised, one hell of a debate," Anderson, who had just come to join them, said. No one argued the point.

"I wonder about one thing. Maybe it will turn out that Shackles looses the big game," Clay suggested. "Paul, Shackles did come to your place?"

"Twice. Once about eight months ago and one about five."

"Who else?"

"Well ... first time only his own guard. He spent the day fishing. Second time was also a fishing trip. He didn't want anyone bothering him. He likes to fish."

Clay nodded and looked grim. They went their separate ways. Tomorrow was the election. It didn't make any real difference who won.

Clay went to the police station in Grandvista for the booking of Boars. He asked for a short off-the-record chat. He wanted to get a few ideas planted in Boars' head.

Then he picked up Tim and headed back to Seaview.

"Gonna tell me?" Tim asked.

"Shackles wouldn't worry about those pictures. Boars has something else. I want him to bring it out. I made it sound like Shackles was behind his arrest one way or another.

"Tim, Shackles won that race, no matter if Boars took the election or not. He can take over Chatters in an afternoon and be in control. There's something a lot deeper here."

Tim agreed. This wasn't over. It wouldn't be until Boars was taken away. Clay was trying to get Boars to spill what he had. There was a deal somewhere in this mess they hadn't found a thing about.

"Face it, Tim. Grandvista isn't worth it. I can't think what it could be."

"And Boars had a boat or two he could use to meet Shackles in the ocean where no one would know. They could go out beyond the range of telescopes or such. They could see anyone who could see them."

"We'll see what comes out."

A Trial

"Prosecution rests. Defense?"

Arthur Cartwright Sylvans III stood, looked at some papers, looked at Boars, shrugged and said, "With the court's agreement, defense wishes for Mr. Boars, who is a qualified attorney, to present an essay style defense. He will, in that statement, admit to the killing of Simpkins."

"Without your objection, prosecution?" Judge Wright asked. Kenwood, the prosecutor, said within reasonable limits, no objection.

Boars stood and went to the witness stand to sit. He quoted the oath, then looked to the jury box.

"I will, as counsel stated, admit that I killed Simpkins. There is no purpose to denying it.

"I wish to present a few little facts for your perusal. This is still a case of politics.

"I was too ambitious. I was a successful lawyer who decided to get into politics for all the wrong reasons. I wanted to get filthy rich, live in a big house, have chauffeured limousines and a private jet to take me all over the world. I wanted every woman who heard my name to want to catch me to make her equally wealthy.

"I didn't care how I managed it, only that I did manage it. In other words, a typical politician, though I thought at the time that I was somebody special.

"I decided to run for a minor office, build it into a state office, build that into a national office and that into president. I laid out the schedule that said I'd be president when I was fifty two years old. That some hundreds of thousands of lawyers had the same plan didn't occur to me for some reason.

"I was approached by a man named Mr. Chatters, who many of you will recognize due to earlier publicities. He had the one thing I lacked. Two things: Contacts and money.

"So it was a crooked deal. Most of them are when it comes to politics. It would get me where I wanted to be.

"I agreed. I would get what I want, Chatters would get a lot more money through graft and corruption. Big deal!

"I filed for candidacy and began my campaign. I was running a strong second to another. I needed a gimmick.

"I was running, at Chatters' suggestion, on an anticorruption ticket. It's a strong running point in a place like Grandvista. Chatters suggested that an attempt to assassinate me would put me a mile over the competition. He also felt that I would need something that would point away from me if anyone tumbl ... figured what I was doing.

"There was a man named Simpkins who looked like a twin brother. How about if I got a lot of pictures of me with known gangsters? There were some pictures like that, but we could make this just good enough that the pictures could be proven false. Simpkins had some very visible features that would show immediately when the photos were blown up. A scar or two. A nick out of his ear.

"Just before this I had a call from a man named Smith who said he had a proposition that I couldn't pass up. I could win the local election, then run for a state job in the next election that would guarantee me national publicity when I started convicting all the corrupt thugs in the state. I was guaranteed that job. State's Attorney!

"I went fishing on a certain date at a certain time. Twenty three miles offshore I met a boat and we sealed the preliminary deal. I met the same boat one other time to finalize the agreement.

"Those meetings were with Georgio Shackles, another name you will know.

"There was a small problem. Simpkins had a set of the pictures to be used in the campaign. He wanted fifty thousand dollars not to turn them over to the present State's Attorney, along with an affidavit that explained his complicity in return for immunity.

"That is blackmail, which means I automatically get a reduced sentence for killing him. It is, in effect, self-defense.

"I decided to use his death in my campaign. 'See? They tried to assassinate me because I won't let go!' It would prove to the public that I'm serious. The others may as well drop out of the race.

"Things started going wrong. I waited too long to report that I had killed Simpkins. Officer Fordham was a lot more intelligent than I'd figured. He wasn't just a rookie in a plush job.

"I was also terrified. Someone actually did try to assassinate me, and while I was with Fordham. I had no idea who it might be. It could be Chatters, but he stood to lose a lot if anything happened to me.

"You see, I have some evidence I was using to keep him in line for Shackles to use when and as he chose.

"I later had it pointed out to me that it could also be Shackles. I had blown the act when I waited so long. It would have worked if I called as soon as I could get to the road. Ten minutes after I shot

Simpkins. I was a danger to him if I had material I could use to threaten him. One does not threaten the Georgio Shackles of this world.

"Now it comes to this. Had Shackles not tried to have me assassinated it would never come out. Now it does.

"I also have some pictures that are not staged. They are of my meetings with Shackles and come with very poor photography, but very good sound.

"Artie? If you will present to the court the items in question?"

Sylvans took a thick envelop from his briefcase to hand to the bailiff, who handed it to the judge. It contained a long statement and two audio-video mini-cassettes. The judge called in a guard and ordered the items secured more strongly than Ft. Knox.

"The defense rests," Boars said. "Plea of guilty with extenuating circumstances.

"Prosecution, your witness."

"Nothing further in this matter."

"The court thanks the jury for its indulgence. A plea of guilty with extenuating circumstances is for the judge, me, to consider at sentencing.

"Court adjourned until sentencing at three PM on Monday." She rapped the gavel and swept out.

They were just getting to their cars to head back to Seaview when Clay's private cell phone buzzed. It was an unlisted number calling.

"Yes?"

"Officer Fordham? This is Georgio Shackles. I just wanted to say that I did not order any hit on Boars – though I should have, apparently. I have no idea who did. I can't see Chatters. He's got too much lost already.

"I'll be gone before they can come after me. I won't ever again be in a place where I can be touched by your government.

"On the chance it was Chatters, who's about that stupid, I will have some things delivered to your office tomorrow.

"Let Johnson run with that job. He might have sense enough to actually get a few of my old competitors out of business. He could turn into a good politician. I think I respect you. I doubt you'll ever know who fired at Boars, but please tell Johnson who it was if you do. Just curious. I don't know what was behind it. Friend Boars won't last a year in prison. Blackmailers don't fare well at all there. Them and pedophiles."

"Maybe, the way I figure it, some other person Boars was blackmailing or something saw an opportunity to scare him into making the mistakes that would can him. It worked."

"Ah, yes! Very possible! He was trying to blackmail everybody around him, so maybe someone found a way to discredit him that would let others off the hook, so to speak! I said I found you intelligent! If it was somebody trying to scare him into getting his ass fried, no need to tell me. I might want to give them a million or so reward – except it went a long way past just him. That's why I'm running.

"Plane's about to take off. Sayonara!"

He rang off. Clay had it on speaker.

Tim said, "That must be what happened! Somebody wanted to scare him into doing what he did!"

That got him the finger.

"... you will serve fifteen years in state penitentiary. It will be to the parole board to determine if there has been rehabilitation enough to shorten that sentence. So stated. Court is adjourned." Judge Collins swept out of the court-room.

"Well, we have Chatters by the balls on the shit he gave us. Shackles is gone. We have no idea where. We'll have an open warrant for him for the next seven years," Clifford Barnes, state corruption board, said. "Johnson doesn't seem so happy with his job, but he'll do it. Skinny is that Shackles told him to play it straight and he'd get the promised backing.

"Have you found who shot at the bastard?"

"Yeah. We won't reveal who. It was someone who wanted to scare him into screwing up. It worked.," Tim answered.

"Yeah. Sleeping dogs and all that. Got to get a bite and head back to Capital City."

"We'll get back to violent crimes and all other departments in Seaview," Clay said. "It seems we have a crime wave in progress. Somebody's painting suggestive pictures on the wall at the cemetery."

"Mustn't allow that to get a start!" Paul warned. "Simple juvenile delinquency at this stage lands them in the pen when they reach eighteen! Mark my words!"

They went on, laughing and joking, each going his own way. Clay, Tim and Janet got back just at lunch time. Mayor Williams was at the restaurant and joined them.

"I'm retiring from this lousy mayor job," he complained. "I had to spend a whole three hours last week with a bunch of lawyers who want to open a lounge and hotel. It would be an expensive whorehouse, you ask me. They hinted that they could allow me twenty thousand dollars if I could expedite the permits.

"I referred them to the corruption board. I think they got the point.

"Lawyers? Naw!"

"Three whole hours last week? That job's going to eat up all your free time!" Janet cried.

"Yeah. That's why I'm retiring for the fiftieth time.

"Clay? Want to run for mayor?"

"No."

C. D. Moulton's works are available on most major outlets as printed or e-books. CD writes the CD Grimes, PI, mysteries, the Det. Lt. Nick Storie mysteries, the Clint Faraday mysteries, the Flight of the Maita science fiction series, books on orchid culture and many others of many types. Mystery, adventure, intrigue, science fiction, humor, fantasy, paranormal, mild erotica, and factual.

www.ingramcontent.com/pod-product-compliance
Lightning Source LLC
Chambersburg PA
CBHW052218150726
48002CB00003B/1168